by **Lauren Thompson** *pictures by* **Derek Anderson**

SCHOLASTIC INC.
New York Toronto London Auckland Sydney
Mexico City New Delhi Hong Kong Buenos Aires

Mama Duck had five little ducklings, Widdle, Waddle, Piddle, Puddle, and Little Quack.

Day was done, and Mama Duck said,
"Snuggle close, and shut your eyes.
It's sleepy time, little ducklings!"

So Widdle, Waddle, Piddle,
Puddle, and Little Quack
snuggled close to Mama.
Then her five little ducklings
saw *blink! blink! blink!*

“Look, Mama, look!” they cried. “What’s that flashing in the dark?”

Mama Duck looked, and then she said,
"Those are fireflies winking 'good night.'
That's what is blinking in the dark.
Now it's sleepy time, little ducklings."

Widdle shut her eyes and went to sleep.
But Waddle, Piddle, Puddle, and Little
Quack were still awake.
Those four little ducklings heard
*whooo! whooo! whooo!*
“Listen, Mama, listen!” they cried.
“What’s that hooting in the dark?”

Mama Duck listened, and then she said,
"That's an owl perched high above.
That's what is hooting in the dark.
Now it's sleepy time, little ducklings."

Waddle shut his eyes and went to sleep.
But Piddle, Puddle, and Little Quack were still awake.
Those three little ducklings saw something
*sway, sway, sway.*
“Look, Mama, look!” they cried. “What’s that moving
in the dark?”

Mama looked, and then she said,
"That's the tree that you play beside.
That's what is moving in the dark.
Now it's sleepy time, little ducklings."

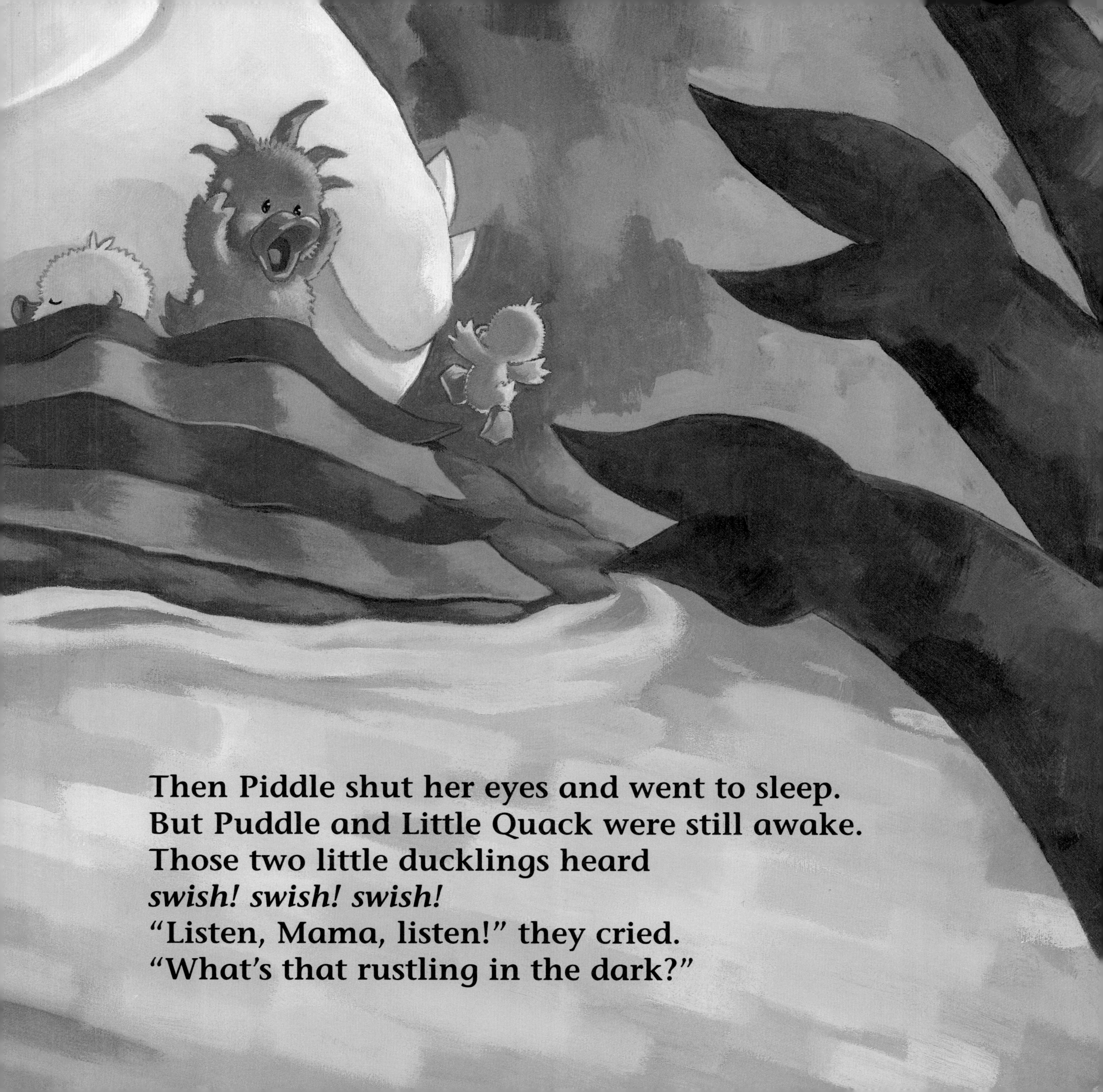

Then Piddle shut her eyes and went to sleep.
But Puddle and Little Quack were still awake.
Those two little ducklings heard
*swish! swish! swish!*
"Listen, Mama, listen!" they cried.
"What's that rustling in the dark?"

Mama Duck listened, and then she said,
"Those are the reeds saying 'hush' to the night.
That's what is rustling in the dark.
Now it's sleepy time, little ducklings."

Puddle shut his eyes and went to sleep.
But Little Quack was still awake.
Little Quack looked. Little Quack listened.
All around was *dark, dark, dark.*

“Mama!” he cried. “Why, oh, why is the night so dark?”

Mama snuggled close, and then she said,
"So the stars can shine their twinkling light.
That's why the night is, oh, so dark.
Now it's sleepy time, little duckling."

Then Little Quack shut his eyes . . .
and went to sleep. . . .

Good night, little ducklings, good night!

Sweet dreams, Cheryl
—D. A.

To Owen, our snuggly
little duckling—L. T.



ISBN 0-439-85619-1

 Published by Scholastic Inc., 557 Broadway, New York, NY 10012, by arrangement with Simon & Schuster Books for Young Readers, Simon & Schuster Children's Publishing Division. 

12 11 10 9 8 7 6 5 4 3 2 1 6 7 8 9 10 11/0

Printed in the U.S.A 08

First Scholastic printing, March 2006

Title hand-lettering by Derek Anderson

Book design by Greg Stadnyk

The text for this book is set in Stone Informal.

The illustrations for this book are rendered in acrylic on canvas.